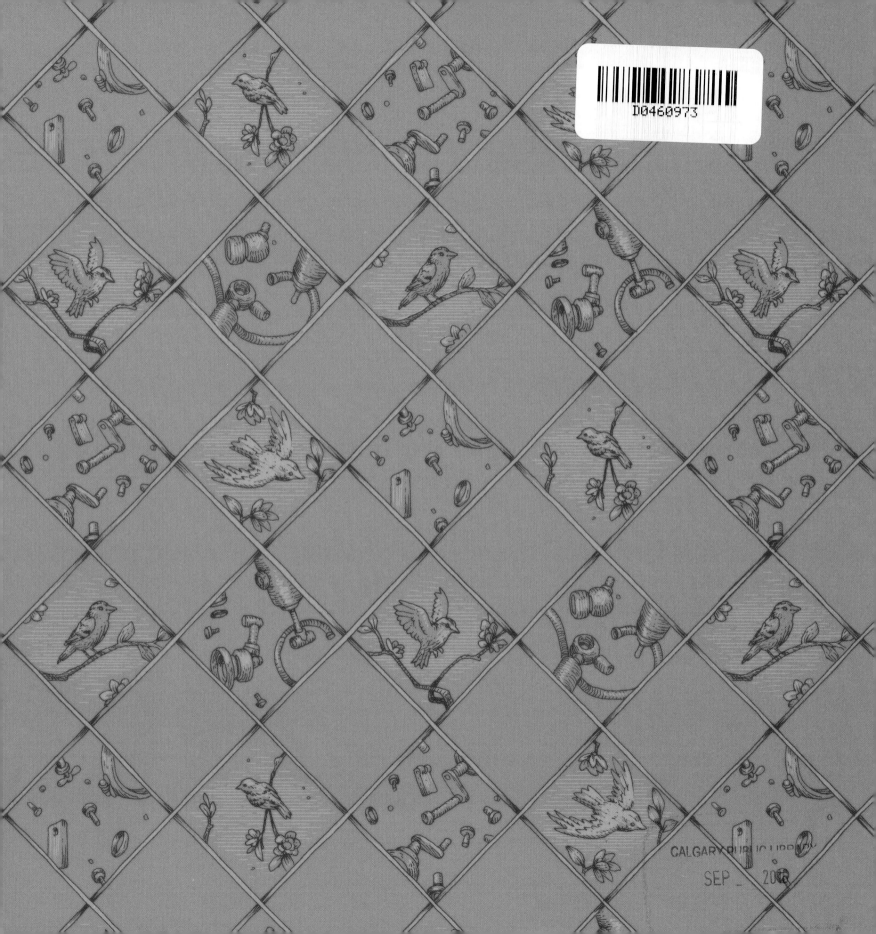

Little Bot
and
Sparrow

Jake Parker

Roaring Brook Press

New York

For Alison

Copyright © 2016 by Jake Parker
Published by Roaring Brook Press
Roaring Brook Press is a division of Holtzbrinck Publishing Holdings Limited Partnership
175 Fifth Avenue, New York, New York 10010
mackids.com

Library of Congress Control Number: 2015034425

ISBN 978-1-62672-367-2

Our books may be purchased in bulk for promotional, educational, or business use.
Please contact your local bookseller or the Macmillan Corporate and Premium Sales Department
at (800) 221-7945 ext. 5442 or by e-mail at MacmillanSpecialMarkets@macmillan.com.

First edition 2016
Book design by Andrew Arnold
Printed in China by Toppan Leefung Printing Ltd., Dongguan City, Guangdong Province

10 9 8 7 6 5 4 3 2 1

One day Little Bot wasn't needed anymore.
He was thrown out with the garbage.

For once, he didn't have
any work to do.

Little Bot lay there for a
very long time . . .

. . . until a flock of birds decided he was the perfect place to perch.

Having never seen a bird before, Little Bot decided to say,

"Hello!"

This didn't go so well.

The birds quickly flew away . . .

. . . but one decided to stay behind.

Sparrow had never seen
a robot before.

Curious, she watched . . .

and watched . . .

and watched . . .

. . . until she realized that the robot just
needed to be taken under her wing.

She led him to the
forest, introduced him
to her friends,

and taught him why robots shouldn't fly.

He learned that not everything
in Sparrow's world was sweet.

Some things had a sting to them.

Other things were better left alone.

And some scary things . . .

. . . were actually beautiful.

Each night, Little Bot watched
Sparrow while she slept.

He once asked her why she needed to sleep.
"To rest and to dream," Sparrow said.

Little Bot didn't know what it
meant to dream.

He decided it was best left for
the birds.

One day, Little Bot noticed the leaves changing.
"Winter is coming," Sparrow said, looking at the sky.

"What does that mean?" the robot asked.
"It means that I'll be leaving soon," Sparrow replied.

As the days went by, the leaves fell and the air became colder.

Little Bot could feel his time
with Sparrow growing shorter.

Then the first snowflake fell.

And they knew it was
time to say goodbye.

Little Bot watched Sparrow until
she was a tiny dot in the sky.

Then she was gone.

Alone again, Little Bot
roamed the forest.

He thought about everything he had learned from
Sparrow and the time they'd spent together.

He wondered if she
was safe and warm.

Little Bot wandered back to the hill where he first met Sparrow.

He closed his eyes, and that night . . .

. . . the little robot dreamed.